Bella Sara™

6

Thunder's Courage

HarperCollins®, ♣®, and Harper Festival®
are trademarks of HarperCollins Publishers.

Bella Sara: Thunder's Courage
Cover and interior illustrations by Heather Theurer
Copyright © 2009 Hidden City Games, Inc. © 2005–2009 conceptcard. All rights reserved.
BELLA SARA is a trademark of conceptcard and is used by Hidden City Games under license.
Licensed by Granada Ventures Limited.
Printed in the United States of America.

For information address HarperCollins Children's Books,
a division of HarperCollins Publishers,
1350 Avenue of the Americas, New York, NY 10019.
www.harpercollinschildrens.com
www.bellasara.com

Library of Congress catalog card number: 2008924827
ISBN 978-0-06-167332-0
❖
First Edition

Bella Sara™

6

Thunder's Courage

Written by Felicity Brown
Illustrated by Heather Theurer

HarperFestival®
A Division of HarperCollins Publishers

1

*S*evi Dahlstrom sat in a room above her parents' silk shop, putting the finishing touches on a beautiful silk gown. Outside, the afternoon sun shone brightly, casting a brilliant glow over Darkcomb Valley.

From her window, Sevi could see in the southwest the striking pink towers of Rolandsgaard Castle stretching high into the sky. Sevi was awed by the magnificence of the castle, which stood at the center of the Trails End estate. One of the things she used to love was riding her horse friend Balin on a long trail that took them past the castle and up into the nearby Whitemantle Mountain range.

I wish I were out riding Balin now, Sevi thought.

Sevi had been just eight years old when Balin appeared in the yard behind the silk shop one warm summer evening. He was a beautiful, gentle horse. His honey-colored coat had gleamed in the softening light, and his hazel eyes had sparkled with warmth and curiosity. When Sevi offered him an apple, he'd gobbled it up, right out of the palm of her hand. Ever since then she and Balin had been inseparable. Together they had explored all the forests, mountains, and villages around Darkcomb Valley.

But a year ago, Balin had fallen and broken his foreleg while jumping over a stream with Sevi on his back. Although she'd done her best to nurse him, the leg was too badly broken to heal. Unable to walk, Balin had weakened and died.

Sevi's eyes sparkled with tears as she thought about her friend. *I miss him so much*, she thought. *If only I'd been able to save him.*

The sound of the door banging open snapped her back to the present. Cody, her nine-year-old brother, bounced in, carrying a mug full of purple berry juice in his hand.

Cody worshipped his big sister. From the moment he could walk, he had followed Sevi around. She had taught him how to ride when he was just five years old, and now he was almost as good with horses as she was. Before Balin's accident, they used to go riding together around Darkcomb Valley and Trails End almost every day. Sevi rode on Balin, and Cody rode on Felix, a tall, rangy, gray-spotted stallion.

Since Balin's accident, Cody kept offering to take Sevi out for rides with him on Felix. She went sometimes, but more often she found excuses to avoid going. She knew that Cody didn't quite understand why, and that he was hurt by her ignoring him. But she couldn't help herself. Being around Cody and Felix reminded her too much of her sadness.

"Hi, Sevi, what are you doing?" Cody asked. Without waiting for an answer, he babbled on, "Want to go for a ride with me and Felix? Let's go for a ride, Sevi. Come on, please!"

Sevi held up her hands. "I'm busy! Can't you see?" she said. Ordinarily she found Cody's enthusiasm sweet, but right now, in her sad mood, she could do with a little less of it.

"Are you still working on that dress? Aren't you done yet?" Cody asked.

"Almost," Sevi told him. "Be careful with that mug, Cody. If you spill juice on my coming-of-age gown . . ."

The floor-length dress she was working on was extraordinary. The design was simple, but it was made from the finest silk in Darkcomb Valley. Into this beautiful cream-colored fabric, Sevi had embroidered intricate patterns in rich golden thread. The embroidery alone had taken her more than five months to complete, but it had been worth it. This was the dress she would wear to her Age Ceremony, after all—the ceremony that marked her thirteenth birthday.

"I won't spill!" Cody protested. He stepped closer—and stumbled over a low stool that was hidden under the folds of Sevi's gown. He pitched forward, and the juice flew out of his mug in a long, shining arc. *SPLAT!* It hit the sleeve of the gown. The purple of the juice almost glowed against the creamy silk.

For a moment both children stood entirely still. Cody's eyes grew as round as two saucers. Then . . .

"CODY!" Sevi screeched.

"I'm sorry, I'm sorry, I'm sorry!" Cody cried. He backed away. "It was an accident!"

"I told you to be careful!" Sevi yelled.

Their mother, Joani, hurried into the room, drawn by Sevi's raised voice. "What's happened? What is wrong?"

Sevi pointed at the juice-splashed silk, fighting back tears of frustration. "Look what Cody did, Mama. My dress—it's ruined!"

"Oh, my," Joani said. She clucked her tongue as she studied the spreading stain. "That is bad."

"I'm sorry!" Now Cody was almost in tears, too. "I tripped. It was an accident. I'm so sorry, Sevi."

Sevi knew Cody meant it, but at the moment she couldn't find it in her heart to forgive him. More than five months of work down the drain. And the Age Ceremony was only three days away!

Tightening her lips, she turned away from her little brother's pleading gaze.

"We can fix it, Sevi," Joani told her daughter. "I don't think we can weave any more of the cream silk before the ceremony—we don't have the right thread in stock. But we can soak out most of the stain. And I can help you embroider over what's left of it."

"What's the point?" Sevi said bitterly. "It won't be right."

Whirling, she ran out of the room and downstairs to the shop. She almost went out to the pasture where Balin used to graze. But then she remembered: He wasn't there anymore. Rushing through the front of the store, where all the family's silk cloth and embroidery work was displayed, she dashed into the stockroom and slammed the door behind her. She stood there for a moment in the dimness, breathing deeply.

The truth was, she knew she had overreacted to Cody's accident. She was overreacting to everything these days, because she was so anxious and upset about the Age Ceremony. The dress was just the last straw.

In Darkcomb Valley, where Sevi and Cody lived with their parents, the Age Ceremony marked the transition out of childhood. Not that you were an adult once the Age Ceremony was over— far from it. But at the ceremony you had to announce what you would study for the next five years. It was a very big decision.

And Sevi was caught between two very different paths.

On the one hand, she was a talented weaver and dressmaker, and she dreamed of becoming a famous designer. And she knew her parents counted on her to stay and help them with their business.

On the other hand, she had a natural ability to care for people and animals. That was what made the death of Balin even harder for her to bear. Since he had gone, she had felt more strongly than ever the urge to follow in the footsteps of Mitka and Sigga Rolanddotter and their fellow Caregivers, who many centuries ago had traveled the land on horseback, caring for the sick and needy. "I owe it to Balin's memory," she had told her parents.

"First of all, you don't owe it to anyone, Sevi. What happened to Balin is terribly sad, but it was not your fault, nor could you have changed it," Sevi's father, Franz, had pointed out. "Second, we need you here."

"Franz," Sevi's mother objected. "Sevi can't be bound by our needs."

But he's right, Sevi thought. *They do need me.* She was already well known in Darkcomb Valley for the clothing she designed and sewed. Her parents sold her creations in their silk shop, and it was an important part of their business.

Franz held up his hands. "All right. But there are other things to consider. Like the fact that there are no Caregivers anymore. The group does not exist."

"I could start a new group," Sevi said stubbornly.

Franz sighed. "And finally, Sevi, you're far too young to roam all over North of North on your own."

"I don't have to start traveling right away," she argued. "I'll wait until I'm grown. But I could start learning about herbs and medicines now."

"It's a fine idea, Sevi," Joani said gently. "The trouble is, there are no skilled herbalists in Darkcomb Valley. You'd have to travel to goodness knows where to find a teacher who could train you. I'm not sure I could bear to let my daughter go so soon! Besides, you have such a talent as a weaver—and you love to make clothing, you know you do. How can you neglect that?"

Sevi had fallen silent. What her mother said was true. She did love to weave and sew. She loved spinning and dying the thread, seeing the way a piece of cloth grew on her loom, planning the embroidery on a bodice or the shape and color of buttons. Making clothes was never a chore.

"We won't dictate what you will choose," her father said. "But think carefully, Sevi. Think about what is truly right and what is truly possible."

How am I going to choose? Sevi thought now. *I don't think I'll ever know which path is the right one.*

As she stood in the stockroom, she heard a voice coming from the store. "Hello? Is anyone here? I need service."

Sevi took a deep breath, trying to calm down. Then she opened the stockroom door and stepped out.

A woman stood fingering one of the bolts of silk in the store. Sevi wondered where her mother and father were. Usually they were on hand to greet customers.

The woman turned, and Sevi felt a slight chill. The newcomer was dressed in layers of gauzy gray that seemed to flow and shimmer like water. She was tall, with a pale, chiseled face dominated by a beaklike nose. Her cold eyes were pale green. The most striking thing about her, though, was her hair. It was white and fine, and it glistened with a sort of rainbow reflection. It didn't look like hair at all, Sevi thought. More like some kind of fine gossamer thread. Also, aside from the white hair, the woman looked young, with no lines or wrinkles on her face.

The woman looked down her nose at Sevi. "Child, do you make garments from the silk of spiders?" she asked. Her voice was deep and slightly harsh.

Sevi blinked, startled. "I'm afraid not, madam," she said politely. "I don't know of anyone who harvests spider silk. They say there's a sorceress living deep within the forest who commands spiders, but I've never seen her. All our silk comes from silkworms."

"Hmmm," the tall woman murmured. "Pity." She ran a long, pale finger down the edge of a length of scarlet silk. Her lip curled into a faint sneer.

"Our silk is of the highest quality," Sevi said firmly. She was irked by the woman's obvious scorn. "My father and mother are both master weavers."

"That may be," the woman replied, "but few weavers, even master weavers, can work with spider gossamer. And no ordinary cloth can match spider silk. It has . . . special qualities."

"Special how?" Sevi asked, curious in spite of herself.

The woman smiled. "Why, spider silk is magical. It gives its wearer knowledge and wisdom far beyond the common range." She held up a gray-clad arm. "I myself wear nothing else. And I see many things. For example, I can see that you carry trouble in your heart. You lost your dearest friend not long ago. And you have a grave choice in front of you, one that will determine the rest of your life."

Sevi gulped. The rest of her life? She hadn't thought of it in quite those terms. But it was true, she supposed—the path she chose now was the one she would have to follow.

"There now, I didn't mean to worry you," the woman said, but there was an edge of mockery in her voice. "Poor child, I'm sure you wish you had some spider silk to help you make the right decision."

Then, without waiting for Sevi's reply, she turned and swept out of the shop.

CHAPTER 2

*O*ver the next couple of days, as she worked to repair the damage and finish her Age Ceremony gown, Sevi couldn't stop thinking about what the white-haired woman had told her.

Was it really true? Did silk made from spider gossamer have the magical power to make its wearer wise?

The woman had seemed wise, that much was certain. She had known about Balin. She had seen into Sevi's heart. Was it really because she wore spider silk?

I wish I had some spider silk to embroider into this dress, Sevi thought. *Maybe it would help me decide which path is the right one. If I choose to stay here and become a master weaver and seamstress, I'll be helping my family, and I'll be doing work that I enjoy. If I study to be a Caregiver, I'll help so many people, and I know I'll love my life—but I'll let my family down.*

Finally, early in the afternoon before the ceremony, the dress was finished. Sevi had promised her family that she would model it for them.

She had spent the morning by herself, going over the embroidery one last time. Now she took off her work clothes and put on the dress. She felt a tingle as she placed her head through the neck opening and let the silk slide down her body.

There was a knock at the door just as Sevi finished buttoning the side of the gown.

"Come in," she called. "I'm ready!"

The door opened and Cody walked in, followed by their mother and father.

"Oh, Sevi, it's magnificent!" her mother exclaimed. "I knew it would be, but when I see you in it, it looks even better than I expected. You've done such a beautiful job. The embroidery is the best work I've ever seen!"

"You do look pretty great," Cody agreed.

Sevi's father walked over to her and took her hand in his.

"You look so grown up, Sevi," he said. "You have a wonderful gift for dressmaking. We are very proud of you. Just make sure you cherish and nurture your talent, and never take it for granted."

Sevi felt the familiar knot in her stomach. "I never will," she promised, "but it still may not be what I choose tomorrow."

"We know it's difficult," her

mother said. "You are right not to take this decision lightly. Is there anything we can do to help you?"

"Well, could you tell me a story? I'd like to hear the one about Mitka and Sigga Rolanddotter and the beginning of the Valkyrie sisterhood." When she was younger, Sevi had loved hearing her mother tell the epic tale.

Joani raised her eyebrows in surprise. "You haven't asked for that one in ages. What made you think of it today?"

"I'm not sure. Maybe because it's about the beginning of the Caregivers."

"Go on, Mama. I want to hear it, too," Cody said.

"Well, all right, I suppose I can tell it once more," Joani said. "But it isn't just about the beginning of the Caregivers, you know. I'll tell you the whole story of Sigga's rise and fall."

She sat down in Sevi's sewing chair. Sevi quickly changed back into her everyday clothes, and then she and Cody arranged themselves on the rug at their mother's feet. Franz headed back downstairs to mind the shop.

"The story starts with Sara, whom we now know as the goddess of horses," Joani began. "But it begins before any of that, when Sara lived quietly with her mother and father. They were gods, but they did not seek to rule. They simply wanted to be at peace with everyone and everything.

"But one day, Sara returned to her home from a day of play to find that both her parents had been killed.

"Sara was overwhelmed with grief, and once she started crying, she could not stop. Centuries passed as she sat in the same spot—the place we know as Teardrop Lake—and wept for the loss of her parents."

Sevi sighed, caught up as always in the sadness of this part of the story.

"Finally, one day, a girl called Sigga and her mother, Mitka, happened by and offered Sara comfort," Joani continued. "They listened to her tale and vowed to take care of her from that day forward. Sara began traveling the land with them. Mitka Rolanddotter was the leader of a group of women known as Caregivers. Their mission was to journey the land performing acts of kindness for those who were in need. They tended to people who were sick, they aided women who were having babies, and they helped survivors to mourn the dead.

"Over time, Sigga and Mitka came to realize that Sara was no ordinary child. As far as they could tell, Sara would never age. She also had a rare bond with horses, which were so drawn to her that she had soon gathered a very special herd. Sara taught Sigga everything she knew about horses, and with Sara's help, Sigga became a skilled horsewoman.

"Sara, for her part, asked some of her horse friends to join with Mitka and her group. On horses, the Caregivers would be able to travel twice as fast and go twice as far to perform their kind deeds. The Caregivers were overjoyed.

"Time passed, and Mitka grew old and passed away. Sigga assumed her mother's role as leader of the Caregivers. It wasn't long before they became powerful and mighty.

"But not everyone shared Sigga's desire to spread goodwill. Soon the Caregivers attracted the attention of an evil woman and her sect of Wolf Riders, who were determined to stop the Caregivers from becoming even more powerful. The Wolf Riders pursued and tormented the Caregivers terribly.

"Just when the end seemed near for Sigga and her women, Sara saved them. She called upon her herd of magical horses, winged and majestic, to carry the Caregivers up and away from their persecutors, past the Auroborus, to a great fortress hidden in the clouds."

"To this day, no one knows exactly

where it is," Cody piped up.

Joani nodded. "In the years that followed, after Sara granted the Caregivers immortality, they became known as the Valkyrie Sisterhood, and each ruled over and looked after a different part of the land. Sigga became the leader of the Valkyrie Sisterhood. She ruled the House of Sigga and all the people, horses, and creatures in North of North for many, many years.

"But at the height of her reign, Sigga faced a difficult choice. She had fallen in love with a mortal, Prince Archer. Although she was forbidden by the Alfather from interfering in the lives of men, when Archer's life was in danger she had to decide whether to follow the love in her heart and save him, or to honor her responsibility to North of North.

"Sigga followed her heart. She and her mortal prince jumped on her golden-winged horse, Valkrist, and flew away together. Although they soon returned, the damage was done. Sigga was banished, forced to leave the beautiful land of North of North behind her. She was also made to give up her seat as the head of the Valkyrie House of Sigga. And Sara's beautiful, mystical horses were scattered across the world.

"And that," Joani said in conclusion, "is the story of Sigga." She looked at each of her children in turn. "Remember this, Sevi and Cody: Choices do matter. Sigga's choice had consequences that lasted the rest of her life and a thousand years beyond it."

Sevi sat in silence for a moment. *Sigga's choice was kind of like mine is,* she thought. *Choose one path, and help many people. Choose the other, and help one person you love. How do you decide something like that?*

"Do you think Sigga did the wrong thing, Mama?" she asked.

"That's a difficult question,"

answered Joani. "I admire Sigga's bravery in choosing to follow her heart. And she did save Archer's life. But she paid a heavy price, and you could also argue that North of North paid a price, too, in losing her. On the other hand, although our world is not perfect, it is a wonderful place the way it is. I think that you will have to make up your own mind about whether or not you think Sigga did the wrong thing."

"I wish Sara's horses were still around in North of North," Cody said, jumping up and galloping around the edge of the room.

"They are," Joani replied. "Or at least, their descendants are. And it's said that the four legendary horses Jewel, Fiona, Nike, and Thunder still roam the land. Sara and Sigga chose them to help protect North of North, you know, and Sara made them immortal so they would always be able to come to the aid of those who most need their help."

"Sevi, don't you think it would be great to ride one of the legendary horses? Especially Thunder! I like him the best because he's a stallion. And he can make lightning come out of his hooves. Wouldn't it be great to ride him?"

"It would be pretty amazing," agreed Sevi. She'd always loved Thunder, too—the striking black stallion with the image of a lightning bolt seared on each flank. Thunder was born of a great storm, and he was said to share in the power of Nature itself. He seemed so strong, so sure of himself.

He'd know which path was right for me, Sevi thought. *If only Thunder could come tell me what to choose!*

Then she had to smile at her own foolishness. A great, legendary horse like Thunder had more important things to do than help a young girl make up her mind!

"He's not exactly Thunder, but . . . do you want to go for a ride with me right now on Felix?" Cody asked, sounding almost shy.

"Go ahead, Sevi," Joani urged. "We've still got preparations to make for the celebration tomorrow, but they can wait until later. Take some time to relax."

Sevi hesitated. What she really wanted was to ride Balin, far and fast, and have some time to herself to think. But she'd had so much time already to think, she realized. And it hadn't really done any good! The ceremony was tomorrow, and one way or the other she'd just have to make up her mind. Maybe at this point it was better not to think about the choice anymore. Maybe if she could stop brooding about it, the answer would become clear.

She glanced at Cody and smiled at his pleading expression.

"Sounds good," she said, and watched his face light up. "Let's go."

A few minutes later, Sevi and Cody

took off toward Trails End. Sevi rode behind her brother on Felix, clinging to his smooth gray sides with her knees and thighs. Felix barely seemed to notice her added weight. And she had to admit, it felt wonderful to be on horseback again, with the wind sweeping her hair back and Felix's powerful muscles bunching and releasing under her.

They galloped through the green, luscious grounds down near Rolands-gaard Castle, and then slowed to a trot when the path became rocky and uneven as they climbed higher and higher toward Mount Whitemantle.

Sevi had told herself she wouldn't think about tomorrow's ceremony dur-ing the ride, but as they approached Darkcomb Forest, the encounter with the strange white-haired woman came back to her.

Darkcomb Forest stood between the foot of Mount Whitemantle and the banks of Horseshoe Bay. Everyone knew the forest was enchanted, filled with all sorts of mythical creatures and wood-folk. The evil sorceress Boda, who ruled a colony of spiders, supposedly lived in its depths, too. The dark tangle of trees was off-limits, but today Sevi felt a strong urge to explore it just a little. What if she could find the spider sorceress? What if she could get just a few strands of spider silk?

She was opening her mouth to suggest they ride in just a little ways, when Cody urged Felix into a canter. He let the horse run until they were well past the turn that led into the trees. Ever since he was a little boy, Cody had been terribly afraid of what lurked inside the forest—especially Boda and her army of giant spiders. Although he always denied it, Sevi knew Cody was scared of spiders, even little ones.

Truth be told, Sevi was also afraid of spiders. Still, she felt a sharp sting of disappointment when Cody moved on.

"Come on, Cody," she said. "Let's go in and look around."

"No way!" he said. "We're not allowed, Sevi!"

"Nobody ever came out and said we weren't allowed," Sevi argued. "I can't believe you're being such a frightened little mouse."

Cody's face flushed and Sevi felt a twinge of guilt. Cody was small for his age, and some of the village children teased him for it, calling him "Mousiekins" and other, crueler nicknames. Sevi knew how much it bothered him.

"Do you really believe all those stories Mama and Father fed us?" she added, trying to change the subject.

"You don't?" Cody asked.

"Well, I guess I believe some of them," Sevi admitted. "But mostly I think they're just trying to keep us from getting lost in the forest. Or maybe Boda's lair is so enchanting, they're afraid we'll find it and never want to come home again!" she added.

"I'm not afraid," Cody said quickly. "It's Felix. He doesn't like the forest, do you, boy?"

Felix let out a snort.

"Ha! Felix isn't afraid of a few spiders," Sevi said. "He can just sense that you are, so he pretends to make you feel better."

"I am not afraid!" Cody insisted.

Sevi let it drop. She felt a bit bad about teasing her little brother. Big sisters were supposed to protect their little brothers, not torment them.

She and Cody continued riding, but neither of them spoke for a while. Sevi could feel all her doubts and tension about the Age Ceremony seeping back.

Eventually Cody broke the silence. "Do you know what path you're going to choose yet?" he asked, a little timidly.

"No," Sevi said, sighing. "I don't think I'll ever be sure. I wish someone would send me a sign of some kind."

"What kind of a sign?"

Sevi frowned. "Well, you know, something odd did happen a couple of days ago. A strange woman came into our shop asking for spider silk." She described her conversation with the white-haired woman. "She said spider silk gives its wearer wisdom."

"She sounds creepy," Cody said, shivering. "What did you tell her?"

Sevi shrugged. "I told her that we didn't have any—that there's only one place I know of where you can get spider silk, and that's from the sorceress of Darkcomb Forest."

"Oh," Cody said. He was silent for a moment. Then he said, "Is that why you wanted to go in there just now? You were hoping to get some spider silk so you could have extra wisdom for tomorrow?"

Sevi nodded. "But it's probably not even true that spider silk gives wisdom," she said with another sigh. "I never heard of it before. It's probably just a myth."

"Probably," Cody echoed.

Sevi glanced up to check the position of the sun. "We should head back," she said. "There's still a lot to do to get ready for tomorrow."

As they rode back toward the valley, the silence stretched between them. Sevi was glad of it. She didn't feel like talking.

"I'm sorry I can't do more to help you with your decision, Sev," Cody finally said.

"What could you possibly do to help me? You're only nine," Sevi pointed out.

"Just because I'm little doesn't mean I can't help," Cody protested.

Sevi reached forward and tousled his hair. "Don't be so sensitive. I didn't mean that the way it sounded, Cody. You know I didn't."

"I guess," Cody mumbled. As they

rode through the lengthening shadows, his face bore a thoughtful, considering expression. If Sevi had seen it, it would have made her wonder what he was plotting. But sitting behind him, deep in her own thoughts, she didn't notice.

3

That night Cody tossed and turned in his bed. He couldn't sleep because he kept thinking about Sevi's Age Ceremony the next day. Cody was worried about her. She'd looked pale and drawn as she helped Joani with the preparations for the big party. Sevi should be happy about coming of age, but Cody hadn't seen her smile once.

I wish I could do something to help her, he thought. *She thinks I'm too little to help. But I'm not. I'm not!*

His thoughts returned to Sevi's story about the strange woman who had come into the shop asking for spider silk. Was it possible that spider silk would really help Sevi make up her mind?

I wish I had been brave enough to go into the forest with her this afternoon. If she just had some of that magical silk, she would be happy.

As Cody lay there in the dark, an idea began to form in his mind. What if he were to get some of the spider silk for Sevi? What if he were to surprise her with it in the morning? She could quickly embroider it into her dress, and then she'd be wise and know what to choose at the Age Ceremony.

Yes. Sevi would be so happy. She'd thank me so much. And everyone would see that even though I'm small, I'm not afraid of anything!

The trouble was, Cody was afraid. Very afraid.

He felt sick to his stomach as he

thought about what he would have to do: ride into Darkcomb Forest, somehow find his way to Boda's secret lair, and capture a few of her spiders to spin for him. And he would have to go tonight. Now.

Moving fast so he wouldn't have time to change his mind, Cody jumped out of bed and began to dress. He tried not to let himself think about the forest and everything that lurked inside its dark canopy. Once he was dressed, he tiptoed down the stairs. He grabbed a glass jar from the storeroom in back of the shop and then headed out into the night.

The moon was full that night, for which Cody was grateful. Surely its bright light would make the forest less forbidding.

Climbing to the top of the low stone wall in front of the shop, Cody whistled the special tune he used to call Felix. In a moment the dappled-gray stallion appeared, trotting up the path toward Cody. His ears were pricked forward in curiosity.

Cody put his arms around Felix's neck and whispered his plan into the horse's ear. Felix snorted forcefully when he understood what Cody had in mind.

"I know it's dangerous," Cody told him. "But I have to do it, Felix. Sevi really needs the silk. And I owe her, for spilling juice all over her gown. And . . . and I want to show her that I can do this, that I'm not just a scared little mouse. Will you help me? Will you come with me?"

In answer, Felix pulled back slightly and gazed at Cody. The horse's eyes were warm and bright. Blowing through his nose, Felix pushed his muzzle gently against Cody's chest. As clearly as words, he was saying, *You know I will always go where you go*.

"Thank you," Cody whispered. Gripping a fistful of Felix's mane, he vaulted onto the stallion's back.

Felix moved at a trot until he was

out of earshot of the village. Then he broke into an easy canter. In half an hour they reached the edge of Darkcomb Forest, where he came to a halt.

Now that they were here, Cody's whole body tensed up. He fought to stave off a surge of panic as all the stories of the forest's strange creatures came back into his mind. There was the one that appeared to be an ordinary, moss-covered fallen log—until you sat down on it and the moss split open to reveal double rows of saw-edged teeth. Or the will-o'-the-wisp, a little dancing light that lured you off the forest paths and led you to who knows where. Or . . .

Cody shook himself. Surely the stories weren't all true. Surely Sevi was right and they were just tales Mama had told to scare him so he wouldn't go wandering off into the forest alone.

Resolved, Cody gave Felix a small nudge, and they entered Darkcomb Forest.

The farther in they went under the great canopy of trees, the darker it got, until there was barely any moonlight peeking through the branches above. The forest was filled with all sorts of rare plant life. Vines seemed to appear out of nowhere and then disappear just as quickly. As he rode, Cody couldn't help noticing gleaming eyes staring at him from all directions—up high, down on the ground, in front of him, behind him—following his every move.

"Keep going. Nothing will hurt you," Cody said aloud, trying to offer himself some encouragement. "All you need is a few tiny spiders. Just remember, you're doing this for Sevi."

"KARRRRKKKK!" Something shrieked, right next to Cody's ear, making him jump in his seat. A blurred shape shot up from the path in front of Felix, and the stallion reared.

"Ahhhh!" Cody yelled, as he slid backward off Felix's back.

* * *

Deep inside her damp, cold cave, the sorceress Boda sat waiting. She could see a clouded image of Cody and Felix in the bowl of magic scrying water set in front of her. She watched as they made their way through the black forest, drawing ever nearer to her lair.

"So it's the little brother who comes seeking a spider for his adored sister! This was not the plan. I meant for *her* to come!" the sorceress said to the hideous creature that squatted nearby. It was a spider the size of a dog, its jointed legs bristling with coarse hairs. Its bulbous body was a sickly grayish white. Its head was dominated by a cluster of shiny black eyes that reflected myriad images of the cave.

"Ugh. So he's a do-gooder just like his sister. Well, I'll put a stop to that. We vanquished the Caregivers a thousand years ago. I won't have them springing up again now."

The sorceress had lived in the

depths of the forest among her spiders for many, many years. Long ago, though, she had been a Wolf Rider, a member of the sect of women who were enemies of Sigga and her Caregivers.

Although she no longer roamed the mountains and plains on wolfback, Boda continued the work of the Wolf Riders from her lair. She had made it her mission to watch the area around Darkcomb Forest and make sure that no one tried to bring back the old ways of Sigga and her sisterhood.

Peering again into the scrying bowl, Boda tapped a finger thoughtfully on her chin.

"Maybe the boy will be useful after all. I will use him to lure his sister to me, and then we'll see how long it takes for both of them to see that my way is the only way."

Cody grasped Felix's mane as the horse reared up, spooked by the strange creature that had just crossed his path. The thing had flown past them so quickly that Cody had only glimpsed batlike features and long, gleaming fangs. He desperately hoped it wouldn't return.

Now, patting Felix's neck soothingly, Cody wondered which direction to take next. In all the stories he'd been told, the sorceress lived in a cave by Fastalon Stream. The trouble was, keeping your sense of direction in the forest was almost impossible. Any time you found what seemed to be a path, it would veer off or end abruptly in a dense thicket of brush.

A twig snapped nearby, and Felix shied sideways. The horse's hide was twitching with nervousness. Cody couldn't blame him. His own scalp crawled, and his head snapped from side to side as he tried to see into the covering darkness.

WHOO! WHOO!

What was that? Cody's heart pounded.

"This is ridiculous," he said out loud. "It's just a night bird. And the snapping twig was probably a skunk, or maybe a tomtomme on its way back to its burrow. Whatever it was, I'm sure it's more scared of us than we are of it, Felix."

Felix neighed.

Taking a deep breath, Cody concentrated on blocking out the eerie forest noises and listened for the sound of running water. After a moment he caught it—a far-off rushing noise. He was almost sure it came from somewhere up ahead to the left. Cody steered Felix in that direction, even though the horse's whole body was rigid with tension and he longed to just turn around and go home.

Felix made his way carefully through the dark forest. Atop his back, Cody tried to ignore the glowing eyes that watched their passage.

A few minutes later, the rushing

sound got louder, and a moment after that, they emerged on the bank of a stream. Cody let out a sigh of relief. Somehow the rushing water seemed less menacing than the dark, twisted trees. Felix seemed to agree, for he stepped into the shallow water and began picking his way downstream. His hoofs clicked on the pebbly bottom. Cody swayed in his seat, lulled by the even rhythm of Felix's footfalls.

The sky had a gray, predawn glow when Cody noticed an area of deep shadow on the right bank of the stream. Peering at it, the boy realized that it was the entrance to a large, rocky cave. Without knowing why, he was absolutely certain that he had found Boda's lair.

Felix splashed onto the muddy bank, and Cody dismounted. Squaring his shoulders, he walked alone toward the dark mouth of the cave. The ground outside it crunched and crackled beneath his feet. Looking down, he was horrified to see that it appeared to be moving! His alarm grew when he realized that the movement was actually thousands of tiny spiders swarming all around him on the forest floor.

Almost panicking, Cody turned back to Felix, desperate to be sitting safely again on his back. The horse neighed, sensing his fear.

No! Cody chided himself. *You have to be brave. You came here to get magical spiders, and here they are—tons of them. So hurry up and get some. You lucked out— you don't even have to go inside the cave and face Boda.*

With that, he pulled the glass jar from inside his jacket and bent down to capture one of the spiders. They moved so quickly, they were almost a blur. They were much harder to capture than Cody had expected. After several failed attempts, though, he finally trapped three of them inside the jar. Relieved, he glanced at Felix. "I did it!" he exclaimed.

In reply, Felix trumpeted a warning and reared up.

Alarm sang through Cody's nerves. He ran toward the horse. Or at least, he tried to. But to his utter terror, his feet seemed to be stuck to the ground.

He glanced down. His eyes widened as he saw that his legs were wrapped in thousands of sticky white strands of spiderweb. A carpet of spiders was streaming up his body, spinning as they ran. Before he could even let out a yell, they had swarmed over his hands and pinned them to his sides.

He struggled with all his might, but the silk of the web was as strong as steel. There was no way he could break free.

And now the spiders were scuttling up his chest. Toward his face . . .

"Felix!" Cody gasped. "Run away! Get help!"

His last glimpse showed him that Felix had turned tail and bolted toward

the stream. Thick ropes of cobweb trailed from the gray stallion's legs and flanks.

And then the spiders wove their silk right over Cody's eyes, and he could see nothing more.

4

The morning of the Age Ceremony was hot and humid. Although the sky was clear, it had a whitish cast that signaled storms were on the way. *The weather matches my mood perfectly*, Sevi thought. *Restless and ready to explode!*

In her bedroom Sevi finished braiding her hair and slipped into her gown. Once the dress was buttoned, she looked at herself one last time in the mirror. She had tossed and turned all night long in her bed, unable to sleep. She still hadn't decided which path she would choose— and the ceremony was only hours away!

What will I do? Should I beg Mama and Father to call off the ceremony? No, I can't do that to them. No one has ever canceled an Age Ceremony. I couldn't bring that shame on the family, she thought. *I'll just have to try to be grown up about this.*

After all, the ceremony was all about coming of age, becoming an adult, and learning how to deal with the things that life would throw at her. In a way, this was her first test.

She looked down at her beautiful dress. Although it wasn't made of spider silk, maybe it could still help guide her, somehow. Maybe once she stepped on to the stage, a decision would just come to her!

She rolled her eyes. *Right!*

There was a soft tap at the door, and her mother walked into the room.

Joani's face lit up with excitement as she gazed at her daughter.

"Sevi, you are the most beautiful girl to come of age whom I have ever laid eyes on. The gown is simply breathtaking! You look like a princess from a fairy tale."

"I wish I was," Sevi replied longingly. She gave herself a mental shake. Time to shed the gloomy attitude! "Mama, where's Cody? I haven't seen him yet this morning. I thought he'd be knocking at my door before the sun rose."

"Your brother, rise before the dawn? Nonsense! I'm sure he's still fast asleep. Come on, let's go and wake him up," Joani said.

They walked down the hall, and Joani rapped loudly on Cody's door.

"Wakey, wakey!" Joani called in a singsong voice. "It's Sevi's big day. How can you be so sleepy with all this excitement going on?"

"Cody, get up!" Sevi added. "I want to talk to you before the ceremony begins." She wanted to apologize to him for being so surly over the last weeks.

Not a sound came from behind the door.

"That boy could sleep through a plague of flame flies! That's it, I'm going in," Joani said, flinging open the door.

"He's not here!" she cried. "Where could he be?"

"I don't know. I haven't seen him since last night. Maybe he took Felix out for an early ride," Sevi suggested. She frowned. Being absent when her big day was here didn't seem like Cody. But then, she reflected, maybe this was his way of showing her his feelings had been hurt by her recent behavior. She bit her lip.

"Well, he'd better get back here soon," Joani snapped. "There's not much time before the ceremony, and I have too much to do to worry about where Cody is."

* * *

Outside, guests had begun to file into the garden behind the silk shop, where the Age Ceremony was to be held. As they took their seats and waited for the ceremony to start, though, the sky began to darken. Storm clouds rolled in from the east.

Ten minutes before the ceremony was due to begin, the sky opened up and rain began pouring down. Lightning flashed and thunder boomed. Joani and Franz hastily carried the food and tables inside. Guests leaped from their seats and sought refuge in the shop, where Sevi had been waiting in a fever of anxiety. Now there would be no magical moment when she appeared before the crowd, radiant in her special gown. But she was so preoccupied, she barely even cared.

Sevi's first feeling when she saw the rain start to pour down was relief. *Now I have a little more time to try to make up my mind. Maybe it will rain all day,* she thought with a burst of hope.

Joani came over to her. "I'm sure this will pass soon," she said in a reassuring voice. "It's just a summer storm, quickly over."

Great, Sevi thought glumly.

Joani stood by Sevi's side a moment longer, her brow wrinkled. "Where could Cody have gotten to?" she wondered aloud, and Sevi heard worry in her voice. "I don't like the thought of him out riding in a storm like this." She grasped Sevi's father by the elbow as he passed by. "Franz, you got up even earlier than I. Did you see Cody? Did he say anything to you about where he was going this morning?"

"I haven't seen him all day," Franz replied, frowning. "And I was up before the sun rose."

Now both Joani and Franz looked decidedly worried. Sevi's stomach clenched. Where could her little brother be?

At that moment, Maan Jakobs the barber, who was peering out the window at the rain, raised his voice. "Franz, isn't that your boy Cody's horse coming down the lane?" he asked.

Sevi and her parents ran to the window, crowding around to peer out. Through the sheets of rain, they saw Felix trotting up the road. The gray stallion's head hung low, and his muzzle was flecked with foam, as though he'd been running hard and was exhausted.

Sevi's heart turned over. "Where's Cody?" she cried. Heedless of the rain on her lovely silk gown, she darted out and ran to Felix. Joani and Franz were right beside her.

As they got close, Sevi could see that Felix's flanks were covered with scratches and cuts. Twigs and leaves were tangled in his mane and tail. Also, he was draped with streamers of some strange, grayish, threadlike stuff.

"Felix, what happened?" Sevi cried.

The horse raised his head and looked at her, his big eyes sad and weary.

"What is this?" Franz muttered, picking a strand of the stuff off of Felix's coat.

"It looks almost like silk," Joani said.

Maan Jakobs, who had followed them out, scraped a handful of the threads up into his palm. "Cobwebs," he announced. "I just swept a mess of them out of one of my cupboards yesterday. It's silk, all right. Spider silk!"

Spider silk? Sevi gasped. Suddenly she knew what had happened to Cody.

He'd gone after the sorceress Boda and her spider silk. And now he must be her prisoner!

"No," she said aloud. "Oh, no. This is all my fault! Oh, Cody!"

The adults turned to stare at her.

"What do you mean?" Joani asked. "Sevi, what is going on? Tell us what you know about this immediately."

"It's my fault," Sevi said again. She felt a sob bubble up inside her. "He went into the forest to get spider silk for me, because of a stupid story I told him. Now he's in terrible danger, and it's all because of me!"

"The forest?" Franz repeated. "You mean he went looking for the sorceress?" He turned pale.

Sevi nodded. "I have to go after him," she said urgently. "I have to save him. He's just a little boy! My little brother!" Turning, she began to hurry down the lane in the direction of Darkcomb Forest. As she ran, she hiked up her ceremonial gown and tucked the trailing hem into her belt.

"Sevi, stop!" Joani cried. "You can't go by yourself! What will it serve if Boda captures you, too?"

That made Sevi halt in her tracks. She looked over her shoulder at her parents.

"We are coming with you," Franz called.

"And so am I," declared Maan the barber.

"And I," old Mr. Onders declared. For the first time, Sevi noticed that a crowd had gathered in the lane, in spite of the downpour.

"Us, too," the Steiger twins chimed in.

Franz looked around at the assembled townspeople. "We thank you all," he said gravely. "We will find Cody together."

The rain let up slightly as the group of searchers from Darkcomb Valley made their way deeper and deeper into the forest. Even in the wet, the woods were alive with eerie shrieks and rustlings. Passing a cluster of oversized forest rats with thick tails and protruding yellow fangs, Sevi tightened her grip on her mother's hand.

"Oh, Mama, what if something really horrible has happened to Cody?" she moaned. "I wish I'd never mentioned that stupid woman and her crazy ideas about spider silk!"

"Sevi, just try to calm down," Joani replied. "What's all this about a woman? And what does it have to do with Cody's disappearance?"

So Sevi told her mother about the woman who had come into the shop last week asking for clothes made from spider silk, and what she had told Sevi.

"I told Cody that I wished I had spider silk because of its magical qualities of clarity and wisdom," she explained. "I thought if I wore something made of spider silk, then I'd be able to decide what my path in life should be. I'm sure Cody came into the forest because he wanted to help me. This is all my fault!"

"I don't know who that woman was," Joani said, "or what she wanted, but I do know she was lying to you about the properties of spider silk. It is indeed strong and durable, but it cannot bring you wisdom. That has to come from within."

"I know, Mama. I realize that now. I'm so sorry. I guess I was just desperate and willing to believe anything," Sevi answered, sadly. "And now Cody's in trouble, all because I couldn't make up my mind on my own."

The party pressed on, tracing the path of the Fastalon Stream. By now the rain had stopped, but the trees still dripped with moisture. Sevi's fine silk dress snagged on countless branches. Twice she slipped and sprawled into the mud. The gown was soon completely ruined. But Sevi would have sacrificed a hundred gowns if doing so would make Cody safe.

A flash of lightning lit up the sky. Moments later, thunder echoed around the forest. Another flash followed, showing the entrance to a dark, gloomy cave on the stream bank up ahead. The party halted.

One of the Steiger twins, bold, brash Trig, suddenly strode forward. He had gone only a few paces when an enormous spider dropped onto his back from an overhanging branch. The creature's hairy, jointed legs were as long and thick as tree branches, and they moved in a blur of speed as the monster began to bundle Trig up into a silken cocoon.

Shouting, Franz and some of the other villagers ran forward. Trig's twin sister, Willa, snatched up a fallen branch and began beating the spider with it. The monster hissed and sprang away, scuttling into the depths of the cave.

They dragged Trig away from the cave mouth, but they couldn't wake him. He lay there, silent and pale, wrapped in sticky layers of web. "The spider must have bitten him," Franz said. "Spiders use their venom to knock their prey out. He needs a doctor."

"Trig, Trig!" Willa cried. "Wake up!"

"We're going to need weapons," Maan said in a low, shaken voice.

"Weapons?" Mr. Onders retorted. "We're going to need the help of the Alfather himself! By Sigga's sword, did you see the size of that thing? Who knows how many more of them there are in that cave!"

Sevi couldn't bring herself to move. All she could see were visions of Cody being snatched up, just like Trig, by a hairy-legged monster and dragged off to his doom.

What if I never see Cody again?

The villagers huddled together, discussing what to do next. Some wanted to go back to Darkcomb Valley and get weapons. Others wanted to send to Canter Hollow, a nearby town, for reinforcements.

Sevi stood there, trying not to scream with nerves and impatience. Cody was in that cave! How were they going to get him out?

Then she caught a flicker of movement in the trees over her head. She glanced up. Her heart almost stopped.

All the trees were alive with spiders! They were about to drop on the humans and attack!

"Look out!" Sevi shrieked, pointing up.

The villagers looked up and saw the threat. Then everyone was screaming and running around madly. Sevi felt something brush against her neck and turned to see a huge spider lowering itself on a web strand behind her. Its legs were waving as it tried to grasp her and bite her.

Sevi let out a scream of terror and took off, running as fast as she could over the tangled vines on the forest floor. She wasn't thinking. She just knew she had to get away.

Twigs slapped her cheeks. Small animals darted out of her path. Finally, exhausted and out of breath, she staggered into a clearing and collapsed in a heap on the ground. Glancing around, she realized that she was far from the spiders and the villagers. She couldn't hear shouting anymore. What was happening to them all?

Laying her head down, she began to sob.

She wasn't sure how long she lay there. She had just raised her head to peer around when an enormous bolt of lightning seared across the sky. There was a sizzling sound and a loud crack. The ground shook, and Sevi covered her eyes in fear.

After the lightning bolt hit, a strange silence fell over the forest. Sevi suddenly felt the presence of some sort of powerful creature beside her. She squeezed her eyes tighter shut.

Gradually, though, she realized that whatever it was did not give off a threatening aura. In fact, she had never felt safer. She opened her eyes.

Standing before her was the most breathtaking black stallion she had ever

seen. His coat shone as if it had been pol-
ished, and his mane rippled like black silk
from the proud arch of his neck. Upon
each hindquarter was the image of a sil-
ver lightning bolt.

Sevi caught her breath. There was
only one horse with those markings in all
of North of North.

Thunder!

*S*evi stared at Thunder in awe. Gazing into his eyes, she felt immediately at ease, as if she had known the legendary horse her whole life.

"It really is you, isn't it?" she said, inching forward slowly. "Thunder?"

Thunder whinnied and stamped his forelegs. As he moved, lightning bolts flashed from his hooves. Sevi was awestruck. And more than that—she felt filled with courage and hope.

"Were you looking for me? How

did you find me?" Sevi asked. Her thoughts whirled, and words tumbled from her mouth. "I can't believe you're right here! Please, Thunder, will you help me save my little brother, Cody, from the spider sorceress?"

Thunder whinnied again and raised his head. Sevi felt a wave of strength from him that was almost powerful enough to touch.

Then, as she stared into Thunder's dark, soulful eyes, a series of images began to race through her mind. The scenes were unfamiliar. They weren't images from her past or future. Sevi sensed that Thunder was somehow transmitting these scenes to her—as if the great stallion were trying to teach her something.

She tried hard to concentrate on what Thunder was showing her. Maybe it would help her figure out how to defeat the spiders and save Cody. She closed her eyes and focused on the images floating through her mind.

She saw a battlefield. A group of men were fighting a much larger army of wolves. The men battled bravely, but they were vastly outnumbered, and the ground was strewn with fallen bodies. Sevi's mouth fell open. She was witnessing the legendary battle between the wolves and the army of mortals led by Sigga's prince! Sevi had heard her mother tell this story so many times, and now she was actually watching it take place before her.

An enormous gray wolf with yellow eyes and dripping fangs fought his way toward Prince Archer. The prince was exhausted. His sword arm, bleeding from many deep bites, hung useless by his side. The beast reared up, ready to attack.

Sevi watched in awe as Sigga herself suddenly descended upon the battle, placing herself protectively between the monstrous wolf and her beloved prince. The Valkyrie maiden wore gleaming battle armor. Her golden hair flowed from

beneath her helmet in two long braids twined with purple orchids. She raised her sword and shield.

And with that, Sevi's mind went blank. The visions had stopped, and she found herself staring back into Thunder's dark, wise eyes.

"Why did you show me Sigga's choice?" Sevi asked him. How odd that Thunder had chosen the exact same story that Sevi's mother had told her only three days earlier!

Thunder looked back at her, his gaze unwavering. Sevi went over the story in her head.

"You're telling me I need to be brave like Sigga," she said. "I'm terrified of Boda and her spiders, but it's my fault that Cody is her prisoner, and it's up to me to save him."

Thunder neighed and shook his mane restlessly. Sevi got the message. They could not afford to wait any longer.

With newfound courage and determination, she swung herself up onto Thunder's back, and they turned toward the heart of Darkcomb Forest.

"Let's go save my brother," said Sevi.

7

hunder let out a ringing neigh. Then he took off, his powerful strides eating up the distance as if it were nothing. The path through the forest was strewn with roots, rocks, and other obstacles. At the speed they were going, Sevi was sure at times that she was about to slide off Thunder's back. But the stallion was surefooted and his gait was incredibly smooth. Sevi eventually relaxed as she realized that Thunder would never let her fall.

Then, rounding a bend, they came upon a group of wood gnomes. Sevi had never encountered these tiny, bark-skinned creatures before, but she recognized them from stories she'd heard. Wood gnomes could travel very swiftly by going through the trunks, branches, and roots of trees. They loved nothing more than to tease and trick anyone who dared to enter the mysterious forest.

Laughing mischievously, the creatures kept popping up through the ground and disappearing just as quickly, creating a circle of holes around Thunder's hooves. Sevi tensed. But Thunder simply reared up and let out a loud, angry neigh. Small lightning bolts flew from his hooves. The wood gnomes let out tiny shrieks of alarm and instantly retreated down into their holes.

There was a pause of a few seconds, and then one of them cautiously stuck its head up above ground.

Sevi cleared her throat and addressed the forest creature. "We are on our way to see the sorceress of the spider colony, and our mission is urgent," she said loudly. "Please show us which direction we need to go. And then get out of our way," she added, her cheeks turning pink.

More tiny heads popped up, and then more. Thunder began galloping around the circle of holes that the wood-folk had created. But this time his anger just seemed to excite the gnomes, who ducked down into their holes as Thunder circled and then popped up again, as if playing a game.

After a few minutes of this, Thunder seemed to have had enough. Stopping short, he stamped his front hooves hard on the ground. Lightning bolts shot out in all directions. Several of them went down the gnome holes, and Sevi heard small, shrill squawks.

A moment later, one of the gnomes surfaced, gave Thunder and Sevi an impish grin, and pointed northeast.

Thunder took off in that direction, with Sevi holding on tightly. She hoped the creature had not played a trick on them and sent them in the wrong direction. Then she heard the sound of Fastalon Stream, and she knew they were going the right way.

There was no sign of Sevi's parents or the other villagers as she and Thunder approached the spider cave. *They must have fought free and gone back to the village for weapons and reinforcements*, Sevi thought.

Two huge spiders stood guard at the mouth of the cave. Thunder drew near warily, ready to fight his way inside if he had to. But the spider guards didn't move.

That's odd, Sevi thought. Her stomach was already tight with dread, but now it clenched up just a little more. "Thunder, I think it's a trap," she said in a low voice.

Thunder nodded his head in agreement. Then he nickered softly. He seemed to be saying, *I know it's a trap. But don't be afraid. I am with you.*

Again Sevi felt that marvelous sense of calm, confident purpose.

Together she and Thunder entered the gloomy cave. Inside, it seemed empty except for hundreds of tattered spiderwebs hanging from the rocky walls. The girl and the horse walked down a narrow tunnel. The silence was eerie, nothing but the ringing sound of Thunder's hooves on the stone floor. The daylight grew weaker and dimmer the farther they went, until at last Sevi could glimpse nothing but shadowy shapes. She sensed rather than saw it when they reached a bigger open space in the cave. Laying her hand on Thunder's warm neck, drawing strength from him, they stepped into the cavern.

There was a faint, swift, scrabbling noise. An instant later, Sevi felt as though someone were sticking thousands of pins all over her whole body. Thunder snorted and stamped his front legs and shot bolts of lightning around the cave.

In one of the flashes, Sevi saw spiders of all shapes and sizes swarming over herself and Thunder, biting at their legs and ankles, scuttling up Sevi's dress and Thunder's beautiful mane. In another flash she saw a monstrous, black, hairy spider lowering its body down from the ceiling over her head. She screamed as she felt the thing's thick legs close around her, pinning her legs to Thunder's flank.

Thunder did his best to fight off the attack, but although he was strong, he was hopelessly outnumbered. The spiders began wrapping webs of sticky silk around Sevi and Thunder. In a very short time, the girl and her horse were bound so tightly together that breaking free seemed impossible.

A sickly greenish light appeared from a tunnel on the other side of the

cavern. As it grew stronger, Sevi could see the clustered, shiny eyes of thousands of spiders, staring hungrily at her and Thunder. Then a tall woman with long white hair stepped into the cave. In one hand she carried a staff. In the other, she held a glowing orb, from which came the greenish light.

The woman walked toward them. The spiders moved out of her way, creating a path. Sevi studied the woman as she approached. That white hair . . . the green eyes and pale face . . .

"You!" Sevi blurted out. "You came into my parents' store asking for spider silk . . . you're Boda, the spider sorceress?"

"I am many things," the woman replied with a cold smile. "In ages past I was a Wolf Rider. I still hold fast to the code of my sisterhood, although my companions these days have eight legs instead of four."

Sevi felt a chill of horror. Boda had been a Wolf Rider? She was part of the group that had tried to destroy the Care-givers!

She must be very old, Sevi realized. And yet, aside from her white hair, the sorceress looked quite youthful, with smooth, unlined skin. She must have powerful magic.

"You are late," Boda said to Sevi in a sharp voice. "I expected you to come searching for spider silk days ago. But instead you hesitated, forcing your little brother to do your bidding instead. Not a good example of your so-called kindness or bravery, is it? It's a shame what I had to do to that poor boy."

"What have you done with my brother?" Sevi demanded. "Tell me. Tell me now!"

8

"Your brother is mine," Boda told Sevi. "And unless you do my bidding, he will remain mine."

Before Sevi could ask what Boda meant, she felt Thunder stir. A furious energy radiated from his body. Then, with a flash of lightning and a loud crack of thunder, the great black stallion burst through the chains of spider silk that bound him and Sevi.

Of course! Sevi thought. *No bond could ever hold Thunder, according to the legends. He had only been biding his time!*

The sorceress's mouth dropped open in shock. Obviously no being had ever been able to break through her magical spiderwebs before.

Thunder was no ordinary being, though. He was one of the legendary horses. His strength and courage were unrivaled, and he would not be bound or held back.

He faced Boda, snorting and stamping. A web of energy seemed to crackle around his glossy black flanks. The sorceress licked her lips nervously, and then quickly retreated several paces. The spiders drew back, too.

"Very well," Boda called, raising her voice slightly. "I will let you go—this time."

"I'm not leaving without Cody," Sevi said fiercely.

Boda let out a single bark of laughter and pointed to yet another opening in the cavern wall. "Your dear brother is in that grotto on the other side of the cave. You may take him, if you really want him."

Overcome with relief, Sevi jumped off Thunder's back and ran toward the grotto. "Cody! Cody!" she called, as she ran.

Behind her, Thunder neighed sharply. *Caution!* the sound urged. He trotted up beside her protectively. Sevi slowed down, suddenly alarmed.

The ground crackled under her feet. She looked down to see the floor of the cave littered with molted exoskeletons, the skins of spiders who'd outgrown them. And some of them were huge . . . bigger than the spiders who guarded the cave.

"Cody!" she called again. Her voice shook. "Cody!"

As she and Thunder inched their way deeper into the cave, Sevi sensed a presence. There was definitely someone in there.

Sevi's caution faded in a flood of joy. "Cody!" she cried again.

Out of the shadows, a dark figure emerged. But it wasn't Cody. It was the largest, most hideous spider Sevi had ever seen! Its swollen body was white with sickly greenish blotches. Its jointed legs, thicker than Sevi's own arms, rose high above its back. Its pincerlike jaws clacked hungrily.

Sevi let out a fearful cry. Thunder stood by her side, strong and alert. When he stamped one forehoof, the creature paused warily.

Outside in the main cave, Boda let out a wicked laugh. "Did you really think I'd make it that easy for you?" she cackled.

With a sudden flash of movement, the giant spider struck, leaping forward and grabbing at Sevi with its monstrous legs. Just as fast, Thunder sent out multiple bolts of lightning. They bounced off the cave walls and shocked the creature back into its corner.

But Sevi was so horrified, she didn't even react to the attack. "What have you done with Cody? Where is my brother?" she asked. Her voice was small and thin.

Once again, Sevi heard Boda's callous laughter. The woman appeared in the entrance.

"Your brother makes a nice addition to my colony, don't you think?" the sorceress said, motioning toward the giant creature.

Sevi's eyes widened as she slowly realized what Boda had just told her. *Has she really turned Cody into that hideous creature?* she thought despairingly. *Could it be a bluff?*

Sevi turned back to the giant spider. Gathering her courage, she stepped toward the creature, pushing away fear and doubt.

"Cody?" she called to the spider. "Is that you?"

"Of course it's him!" Boda sneered. "He dared try to steal my spiders. This is the price he had to pay. And now he's yours—if you still want him."

Sevi looked to Thunder with tears in her eyes. "Is this true?" she pleaded. "Can it be?"

Thunder gazed steadily back at her. *Courage,* his eyes said. And Sevi knew without a doubt that this time Boda was speaking the truth.

She thought her heart would break as she stared at the monster Cody had become. *What can I do?* she thought. *How can I save him?*

The vision of Sigga standing between her prince and the giant wolf flashed into her mind, and Sevi finally understood. The time had come for her to prove her courage. Like Sigga, she needed to trust herself and rise to the challenge. For once, Sevi knew exactly what she had to do.

She took a deep breath. Then she

moved a step closer and spoke to the creature exactly as she wanted to speak to her little brother.

"Cody, it's me, Sevi! Your sister! Don't you remember?"

The giant spider's jaws clicked open and shut, open and shut. It watched Sevi, but it was impossible to read expression in its cluster of black eyes.

"Today was my Age Ceremony, and I couldn't decide which path to choose. So you tried to help me." Sevi took another step forward. "And this dress, I made it for the ceremony!" She held up a fold of torn, muddy silk. "It got a little dirty," she added with a shaky smile.

Click-clack, click-clack went the monster's jaws.

"Mama and Father say that I have a gift for dressmaking and that I shouldn't throw it away," Sevi continued. Did the spider even understand what she was saying? She could only hope she was getting through. "But you know how much I also want to become a Caregiver and follow in Sigga's footsteps."

The sorceress let out a disgusted snort. "Worthless do-gooder," she spat.

Ignoring her, Sevi continued speaking to the spider. "Oh, and Felix is fine, don't worry! He came back to the village to get help after he lost you. That's how we knew where to find you."

At the mention of Felix, the spider's jaws stopped working. Sevi knew then that somewhere inside that monstrous creature, Cody lived.

"You *do* remember!" she cried. "Remember the day you first saw Felix trotting along the road on his own? You went up to him and gave him a carrot, and he nuzzled up to you. It was a perfect match! Then he came home with you, and I gave you your first riding lesson, remember? You and Felix were best friends from the very first moment."

"Sentimental nonsense," Boda

sneered. "Attack!" she commanded the huge spider. But the creature just squatted there, staring at Sevi, who kept talking.

"Cody, look! Look who came to help me. It's Thunder! He came to help me find you, and he showed me so many wonderful things, I can't wait to tell you all about it. Thunder gave me the courage I needed to come here and find you!"

Suddenly, the swollen outline of the spider seemed to blur. For an instant Sevi thought she saw her brother's brown eyes instead of the hideous cluster. The curse was wearing off. Cody was fighting the spell!

"Cody, I love you so much," Sevi blurted out. Her words tumbled over one another. "I'm so sorry I made you think that you had to come here and get me spider silk, just to prove yourself. I'm sorry I teased you and said you were afraid! You are the bravest boy I know!

I couldn't ask for a better brother. You have to come back, Cody. Come home with me. We'll find a way to break the spell on you. We'll find a way to make you a boy again. We'll work it out, somehow. Just come home!"

The giant spider slowly crept out of its corner. Sevi tensed, forcing herself not to shiver as it approached her. Would it attack?

No! It crawled past her, its eight feet clicking faintly on the rocky cave floor. At the entrance to the bigger cave, it paused as if waiting for her.

Sevi's heart soared. Thunder gave a soft, approving snort and moved to stand close to her. Sevi put her hand on the black stallion's arched neck.

Then Boda strode forward to block Sevi's path.

"I'm taking my brother home," Sevi told the sorceress. Although she was shaking inside, her voice was firm. "You've lost, Boda. Love and goodness will always triumph over evil. Now step aside."

"Not so fast," Boda snarled. "Do you think I'm just going to let you walk out of here?" Behind her, rank upon rank of spiders were massing, their jaws working hungrily.

"What do you want?" Sevi asked. Her grip on Thunder's mane tightened. "What will it take for you to let us leave?"

"I want you to join me instead of those pathetic Caregivers," Boda replied. "Swear loyalty to me, and I will make you my apprentice. Why do you think you are such a talented weaver and seamstress? It's because you have a gift like mine. You too could control spiders if you chose. Think of the power we could wield—if only we worked together!"

Finally, Sevi understood. This was what the sorceress had wanted all along. She had been a Wolf Rider, and the Caregivers were her sworn enemies. No matter that the battle had been fought a thousand years ago, Boda still held on to her ancient hate. She would obviously stop at nothing to defeat her foes and rebuild her own power.

Sevi thought again about Sigga and her bravery. She thought about Cody and his love for her, and she thought about Thunder's nobility and courage. Sevi could never turn her back on everything they stood for.

"I won't do it," she said defiantly. "You can keep me prisoner here for as long as you like, but I will never become one of your kind."

As she spoke, a vision flashed through Sevi's mind. She saw herself riding Thunder back down the cave tunnel and out to freedom. Thunder had sent her the vision, and Sevi knew immediately what he meant by it.

"Run!" she shouted to the giant spider. Grasping Thunder's mane, she vaulted up onto his back.

Thunder reared up. His hooves

lashed out and struck Boda. She fell to her knees.

"Get—!" the sorceress began to screech. But the words never left her mouth. As Sevi watched in amazement, Boda's eyes rolled up in her head and she slumped sideways. Crouching behind her, the giant spider's body flickered like a flame. Sevi could see, in flashes, Cody's touseled dark hair, his rosy, rounded cheeks. His mouth seemed to be open in a silent shout.

And then, like hot wax, the hideous, blotchy body melted down onto the cave floor, and Cody stepped out in his familiar boy's form.

"Cody!" Sevi cried, almost weeping with joy. She reached out her hand to her brother and pulled him up to sit behind her on Thunder's back.

Cody gasped. "Sevi!" he said in an awed whisper. "Is this who I think it is?"

"Yes," Sevi confirmed. "I'll explain

later. Let's get out of here, Thunder!"

The great stallion leaped over the unconscious sorceress and out into the large cavern, where the army of spiders blocked their way. Thunder didn't falter for a second. He charged forward, barreling through a row of dog-sized brown spiders. Lightning flew from his hooves and bounced off the cave walls, stunning many more spiders.

Sevi yelled like a wild thing, and Cody joined in. Their whoops seemed to give Thunder fresh energy. Leaping clear over a wave of spiders, he galloped down the long tunnel toward the cave's entrance. In a moment they emerged into bright sunshine.

They were free!

Thunder galloped away from the cave, his stride tireless and joyous.

"Woo-hoo!" Cody yelled gleefully. "We did it! And I can't believe I'm actually riding Thunder!"

"Isn't it the most amazing thing?"

Sevi agreed. "He came to help me rescue you."

"Thank you, Thunder," Cody told the great horse.

"I know the spell on you was broken when Boda got knocked out," Sevi said, as they raced along. "But how did Boda get knocked out? Thunder's hooves hit her on the shoulder, not on her head."

"I bit her," Cody explained with a grin. "Spider venom knocks its victims unconscious. I thought she needed a taste of her own medicine."

Sevi laughed out loud. "Brilliant!" she told her brother.

Thunder let out a neigh that sounded like a laugh. As they rode through the forest, it didn't seem as frightening or dark to Sevi as it had before. Now that she had Thunder and Cody, maybe nothing could ever frighten her again.

CHAPTER 9

As Thunder approached the village, Sevi spotted a group of people hurrying toward them. It was her parents and the villagers, returning to Boda's cave with weapons.

Cody and Sevi hopped down from Thunder's back to hug their parents. Joani burst into tears of relief and happiness. The rest of the villagers cheered. They were thrilled to see the children safe. They were also very glad they wouldn't have to fight the sorceress and her spider army after all!

"Is everyone all right?" Sevi asked anxiously. "Did the spiders harm anyone besides Trig?"

"They got Mr. Onders, too," Franz told her. "Knocked him out with their venom. But we've called in the doctor from Trails End, and it looks as though they'll both be all right."

Thunder's presence caused a great deal of excitement. All the villagers had grown up hearing about the legendary horses, but none had ever seen one before. Thunder stood among them, proud and majestic, dipping his head graciously as people brought their children over to stroke his mane. Again and again, Sevi told the story of how he'd found her in the forest and how she and the stallion had together rescued Cody and defeated Boda, the spider sorceress. The celebrations lasted until late into the night, and when Sevi finally fell into her bed, she was so exhausted, she was asleep before she could even pull the covers up.

With all the excitement, of course, Sevi's Age Ceremony had to be rescheduled. What's more, Sevi quickly had to make up a new dress to replace the one that had gotten ruined in the forest.

For the next six days, Joani frantically prepared more cakes, pastries, and other delicacies, while Sevi once again locked herself in the sewing room above the shop, creating a brand-new coming-of-age gown. Thunder had left them the morning after the rescue, and although Sevi was sorry to see him go, she knew that the magnificent horse would be her friend forever. If ever she needed him, he would know it—and he would come.

"Thank you, Thunder," Sevi whispered to him, as they said their farewells. "I'll never forget what you did for me. Not only did you save Cody, but you taught me to have courage and faith in myself. I will always remember that."

Then she had watched as Thunder galloped away into the early morning mist.

As she stared out the window now at the streets of her small, quiet village, Sevi thought about all she had been through in the past week, about how much she had learned, and about the things she still hoped to discover.

Her thoughts were interrupted by a knock at the door.

"Come in!" Sevi called.

"How's the dress coming along?" Cody asked, bouncing in.

"It's almost done. How's Felix? You've hardly left his side since you got home."

"He's okay. I think he was a little worried I would forget about him after I rode Thunder," Cody said. "I would never do that, of course, but still—don't you think it's amazing that we had that

adventure with Thunder, Sevi? You know what? It was almost worth being turned into a giant spider."

"Stop it, that's not funny!" Sevi scolded, but she couldn't help grinning.

"All right. But, seriously, my adventure in the forest did buy you a whole extra week to make up your mind," Cody said. "So, have you?"

Sevi smiled. "I think so," she said.

"Really?" Cody's eyes widened. "Which path will you choose?"

Sevi's smile broadened. "You'll just have to wait and see," was all she would say.

At last, the day of the second Age Ceremony arrived. Sevi and Joani were alone in Sevi's room. Joani buttoned the last button on Sevi's plain blue silk gown.

"Well, this time the ceremony is definitely happening!" Joani said. "Are you nervous?"

"You know what's funny?" Sevi

said. "I couldn't be calmer. I guess after last week nothing will ever scare me again."

"And it also helps the nerves when you know which path you intend to choose, doesn't it?" her mother asked.

"Yes, I suppose that does help, just a little," Sevi said, laughing.

"Well, it's time. The dress is beautiful, Sevi, although I know it's not the one you hoped you'd be wearing."

"Actually," Sevi said, "I think this dress is perfect. The other one was a bit too fussy, don't you think?"

"Definitely," Joani agreed.

As Sevi walked down the pathway toward the stage, the villagers stood and stared in awe. She wasn't wearing the dress they had whispered about for months, but no one seemed to mind. For everyone knows that it's not the dress that makes the young woman; it's the young woman who makes the dress.

It was customary for the parents

to officiate over the Age Ceremony, welcoming their children into the world as a young adult, ready to make her own way and stand on her own two feet. Joani and Franz stood in the center of the stage. Off to the side stood Cody, looking proud as his sister made her way up the steps.

"My dear daughter," Franz began, "it is time to welcome you into adulthood. We have bestowed upon you wisdom, guidance, and love, and we can only hope that this has helped lead you in your choice. We know that no matter which path you choose, you will do great things, for your heart is true, and that is the most important thing of all."

"Have you chosen your path, dear Sevi?" Joani asked.

"I have. Mama, Father, for years I studied silk weaving and dressmaking, and I love the creations I have made. I also love being part of the family business, being able to create and build something together with you.

"But you know that I have also longed to follow in the great Sigga's footsteps and become a wandering Caregiver, as she was.

"I've struggled with this decision for months; not knowing which path I should choose. And then, last week, I had the privilege of meeting the great horse Thunder, and he showed me visions that taught me how important it is both to cherish the gifts and talents you are born with and to believe in your convictions, no matter what the consequences.

"And so, after thinking about what Thunder taught me, I have decided my choice is not to choose. Instead, I wish to follow both paths. It took courage for Sigga to follow the love in her heart, even though she knew she would face a terrible punishment for doing so. And I admire her for that. But perhaps she also should have been more careful with her powers. There must be a way for me to cherish my powers *and* follow my heart. I don't have to make a choice to follow one path or the other, like Sigga. So I've decided that I will stay with you and continue weaving and dressmaking, as it is a gift, and I do not want to take it for granted. Besides"—Sevi grinned—"staying close to home gives me the opportunity to keep an eye on my little brother, who tends to get himself into trouble!

"However, I also intend to follow my love of Caregiving by studying healing. I hope eventually to offer my services to those in need all over North of North! This, Mama and Father, is my choice."

After a long pause, Joani and Franz both put their arms around their beloved daughter, as the crowd applauded loudly.

"My darling," Joani said, wiping her tears. "You have a lot of work ahead of you, but I believe you can be everything you want to be. You are truly gifted, and you have proven that you really are coming of age!"

With that, the crowd cheered, and the formal ceremony was over. The guests gathered under the canopy to eat and celebrate.

Sevi stood a little back from the crowd, nibbling at a chocolate-filled pastry and savoring the feeling of contentment in her heart. She knew the choice she had made would not make for an easy life. It would be hard work, learning about healing *and* dressmaking, trying every day to prove to herself and her family that she could handle the weight of both of these paths. But she knew, too, that although it took her a long time to come to this decision, she would never turn her back on it.

That night, for the first time in months, Sevi climbed into bed knowing she would sleep peacefully.

Just as she was about to fall asleep,

a loud crash of thunder sounded and lightning flashed in the sky outside. Sevi smiled. She had a feeling that Thunder approved of her decision.

The black colt let out a snort of surprise and pawed the ground. The pale filly spooked and spun, running a few strides back the way she'd come. But the violet filly took a step forward, eyeing Lorelei curiously.

"Hello," Lorelei said, looking directly into the filly's amethyst eyes. "My name is Lorelei. I liked your song."

The filly merely stared for a long moment. Lorelei held her breath, not sure what would happen next.

Then the filly tossed her head, and the floating lyre began to play again. The tomtomme scampered forward and began keeping time with his tail.

Lorelei began to hum along. Part of her wanted to fall into the music and never return. Hearing her voice mingling with the filly's lyre, she felt as if she'd finally found what she'd been seeking.

But another part struggled against the song, although she wasn't sure why. Suddenly, words flooded into her mind, matching the melody. She couldn't resist opening her mouth to sing:

> *The lyrics seem to come to me,*
> *Just like a distant memory;*
>
> *I gladly sing the melody*
> *To add to your sweet harmony;*
>
> *To sing with you I must agree*
> *Our music is a jubilee,*
>
> *With each note played so carefully,*
> *The way sweet music ought to be;*
>
> *For I will sing the melody,*
> *And you will be my harmony.*

As she sang, Lorelei drifted up the hillock to join the foals. The white filly had returned, and both she and the colt danced along with the music. From where she stood, Lorelei could see the whole of the meadow stretching before her. Grazing in the distance was a small herd of adult horses—these foals' parents, she guessed. A rose-pink unicorn and a proud, black, winged unicorn. A creamy white horse with blue beads in her mane and a black horse with a leopard-skin cape. A glistening lavender-maned mare and a golden stallion.

As the song ended, Lorelei found her gaze lingering on the peaceful herd. Seeing them there made her feel happy and sad at the same time. Horses were everywhere in North of North, of course, but Lorelei rarely had the chance to interact with them.

Really? she thought, catching herself. *Wait, how do I know that?*

Just then the lyre finished with a flourish, and the violet filly let out an approving neigh. The colt kicked up his heels with joy, and the pale foal perked her ears happily.

The musical filly took a step forward. Lorelei gasped as her mind suddenly flooded with vivid images. After the uncertainty of her memory loss, it was enough to make her knees buckle. She nearly fell to the ground. The filly jumped back, startled by the reaction, and the images suddenly blinked off.

"No!" Lorelei cried. "Please. It's all right. I was just—just surprised, that's all."

She realized now what had happened. Horses in North of North could communicate with humans by projecting images into their minds. Lorelei knew that such magic happened all the time. Even without most of her memories, however, she was quite certain this was the first time it had happened to her.

The filly lowered her head cautiously. The images came again, more slowly this time. Lorelei focused on the vision the filly was sending her: It was a slender, brown-haired girl. She gasped as she recognized . . . herself! She appeared to be singing, although no sound came from her mouth, only a stream of blue, like a beam of light. Then another stream appeared from some unseen singer, this one as green as a forest glade. The two streams joined and intertwined, forming a beautiful visual duet.

"I get it!" Lorelei blurted out. "Harmony! You're telling me your name is Harmony?"

The filly tossed her head, and the lyre emitted a string of sparkling notes. Lorelei grinned.

"Harmony," she repeated. "It's the perfect name."

The unicorn colt barged forward,

snorting impatiently and pawing the ground. Lorelei smiled, guessing that he wanted to share his name next. Before long, they were all acquainted. The black colt was known as Dart. The pale filly was Moonsprite. Harmony even sent images into Lorelei's mind to introduce the tomtomme, whose name was Bongo.

"It's nice to meet you all," Lorelei said. "I wonder if your parents would mind if I stayed with you for a while. You see, I seem to have forgotten . . . to have forgotten . . ."

Harmony tilted her head quizzically as the girl's words trailed off, but Lorelei hardly noticed. She'd just caught the faintest whisper of some distant melody, carried to her by the night breezes. The voice was beautiful, although plaintive and weak at the same time.

Lorelei gasped as more memories came flooding back. She'd heard that voice before, many times. "It's Serena!"

she cried. Finally noticing the foals' curious stares, she tried to explain what she thought she had heard. It was difficult, though—she could hardly understand any of this herself. "My sister. I can hear her singing. I think—I think she's in trouble. I have to find her!"

She turned and rushed back the way she'd come. She'd hardly gone three steps when the pounding of small hooves surrounded her, nearly drowning out the faint sound of her sister's voice. The foals had caught up to her, Harmony in the lead.

"You believe me? Really?" Tears came to Lorelei's eyes as Harmony flooded her mind with more images. "And you'll come with me? Help me find her? Oh, thank you!" Then she hesitated, remembering the terrifying yellow crow. "But are you sure? It could be dangerous. Your parents . . ."

Dart snorted, rearing up defiantly.

Harmony stamped one foot. Bongo smacked the ground firmly with his tail. Even Moonsprite cast only one nervous glance toward the distant herd before stepping forward. Despite her worry, Lorelei smiled faintly.

"All right," she said. "I suppose we'll be back before they notice. It isn't far."

She blinked, wondering how she knew that. But there was no time to waste on such thoughts. The foals were already trotting ahead toward the edge of the forest. Tilting her head to catch the faint sound of her sister's voice, Lorelei hurried after them.

Go to
www.bellasara.com
and enter the webcode below.
Enjoy!

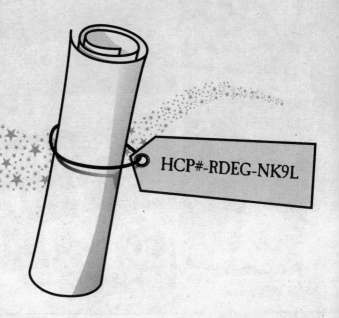

HCP#-RDEG-NK9L